THE AMAZING SPIDER-MAN

HarperCollins®, 🐾®, and HarperFestival® are
trademarks of HarperCollins Publishers.

The Lizard's Legacy
© 2009 Marvel Entertainment, Inc., and its subsidiaries.
MARVEL, all related characters and the distinctive
likenesses thereof: ™ & © 2009 Marvel Entertainment, Inc.,
and its subsidiaries. Licensed by Marvel Characters B.V.
www.marvel.com. All rights reserved.
Printed in the United States of America.
www.harpercollinschildrens.com
Library of Congress catalog card number: 2008937122
ISBN 978-0-06-162627-2

Book design by John Sazaklis
09 10 11 12 13 LP/CW 10 9 8 7 6 5 4 3 2 1
❖
First Edition

THE AMAZING SPIDER-MAN

VOLUME **3**

THE LIZARD'S LEGACY

WRITTEN BY
MARK W. McVEIGH

ILLUSTRATED BY
JOHN SAZAKLIS

HarperFestival®
A Division of HarperCollinsPublishers

PROLOGUE

PETER PARKER WAS JUST AN ORDINARY HIGH SCHOOL STUDENT—UNTIL HE WAS BITTEN BY A RADIOACTIVE SPIDER AND HIS LIFE CHANGED COMPLETELY. PETER DEVELOPED SUPERHUMAN STRENGTH AND A POWERFUL INNER SENSE THAT PROVIDED HIM WITH EARLY WARNING OF DANGER. LIKE A SPIDER, HE COULD CLING TO MOST SURFACES, CRAWL OVER WALLS, AND SHOOT WEBS.

PETER PARKER HAD BECOME . . .

THE AMAZING SPIDER-MAN

PETER PARKER KNEW SOMETHING WAS WRONG as soon as he opened the door to Dr. Connors's laboratory. The room was a mess. Chairs were overturned and chunks of plaster had been smashed out of the walls. Deep claw marks in the columns went from one end of the room to the other. Scientific instruments, chemicals, and files were scattered everywhere.

"What on earth!" Peter exclaimed, as he stared at a jagged hole in the wall where a window used to be.

Peter had been coming to the lab a couple of times a week for the last couple of years to help Dr. Connors with his research. Dr. Connors was a well-respected scientist, so it was a great arrangement for Peter, who was studying science at Empire State University. Peter had learned a lot from the usually calm and intelligent scientist.

Now Peter looked around the lab and saw a notebook lying open on the lab table. The book was torn to shreds, but he could just make out the words *Partim Lacerta* on one of the remaining pages.

That's Latin, Peter thought. *I'm pretty sure it means 'part lizard'.*

"Trust Dr. Connors to write his notes in Latin so hardly anyone can understand them," Peter muttered to himself. "That's just like him. I wonder what he was trying to do, anyway."

Dr. Connors had put a note in the margin in English. *Could this give a human all the good and none of the bad? Too dangerous?* it read.

Sifting through the other papers scattered on the desk, Peter found a letter from the president of Empire State University. The letter was dated two days earlier.

Dear Dr. Connors, the note began, *we are sorry to inform you that we cannot continue to fund your experiments in reptile research. We suggest you close your lab by the end of the semester, as we can no longer be responsible for your expenses.*

That's a big blow for Dr. Connors, Peter thought. *The only things that matter to him are his work and his son, Billy.*

To most people, Dr. Connors was just an ordinary scientist. But Peter wasn't most people. As well as being Peter Parker, he was also Spider-Man. And Spider-Man knew what could happen if you made Dr. Connors angry.

Years ago, Dr. Connors had lost his arm in an accident. Since then, he'd made it his mission to devise a formula that would make his arm grow back. Connors became an expert in reptile science because reptiles are the only creatures that can regrow their limbs.

Finally, two years ago, Dr. Connors figured out a formula that he was sure would grow back his arm. The formula was based on a chemical extracted from lizard blood, and it worked. Unfortunately, as well as growing back Dr. Connor's arm, the formula had a nasty side effect: It turned him into the Lizard.

The Lizard was a nasty seven-foot-tall reptile with powerful arms and legs, a gigantic tail, and hideous green scaly skin. He had superstrength, as well as the ability to control other reptiles with his mind. Worst of all, he disliked all warm-blooded creatures, especially humans.

When Dr. Connors first turned into the Lizard a couple of years ago, Peter had discovered an antidote to change him back into his human form. The antidote had worked, but only temporarily. Now whenever Dr. Connors got really angry or stressed, he turned back into the Lizard.

Looking around the lab at the broken instruments and scratched columns, Peter guessed that the Lizard was back—again.

Suddenly, Peter's spider-sense kicked in. Danger was on the way. He quickly slipped into the closet and put on his Spider-Man suit.

Stepping back into the room, Spider-Man saw crocodiles, ten-foot-long snakes, a huge Komodo dragon, and thousands of small lizards flooding into the laboratory.

I've got nothing against ugly, scaly creatures, but this is ridiculous, Spider-Man thought. *The Lizard is definitely back. Only he can control reptiles like this.*

A cobra slithered up Spider-Man's ankle. He pinned it to the floor with one blast from his right web-shooter. Then, leaping out of biting range of the angry Komodo dragon, Spider-Man scaled the wall and perched on the ceiling. He looked down at the reptiles swarming below him.

I can't exactly leave them here for the janitor to clean up, Spider-Man thought. He shot dozens of web-lines from his shooters, constructing a cage around the larger reptiles. Then he sprayed a fine mist of webbing over the smaller lizards, pinning them to the floor.

"Time to call in the experts," Spider-Man said, as he dialed 911. *I have an even bigger reptile problem to deal with.*

Just as Spider-Man hung up the call, his cell phone rang. It was J. Jonah Jameson, publisher of the *Daily Bugle* newspaper, where Peter Parker worked part time as a photographer.

"Parker, it's Jameson," his boss shouted. "Get in here now. There's a big story breaking. Big and slimy!" *Click.*

Spider-Man sighed. *It's not easy having two lives,* he thought. *But I might as well get some shots for Jameson while I'm here.*

He jumped down from his perch and set his camera on auto-timer. Spider-Man rewebbed the reptiles as the camera automatically took shot after shot of him in action.

That should keep Jameson happy for at least five minutes, he thought. His boss was always asking for more photos of Spider-Man in action.

Once he had enough pictures, Spider-Man slipped back into his street clothes and set off for the *Daily Bugle.*

Moments after Peter had left the lab, the Lizard's clawed hands appeared at the bottom of the hole in the far wall. Bricks and plaster flew everywhere as he hauled his huge

The Lizard's yellow eyes flashed with anger.

body into the room through the opening. The Lizard's yellow eyes flashed with anger. He immediately began ripping apart Spider-Man's webbing.

Once he'd set all the reptiles free, the Lizard stomped toward the door. Banging his enormous tail back and forth, he smashed the doorframe on both sides so all the reptiles, from the smallest to the largest, could crowd out behind him. The Lizard had a plan, and his fellow reptiles were going to help him.

CHAPTER

AT THE DAILY BUGLE, JAMESON WAS pacing the floor of his office.

"Do you have any idea what's going on in this city?" he shouted at Peter. "Because I sure as heck don't."

"Hmmm, let me guess," Peter answered. "I know! There's a huge pack of reptiles on the loose."

Jameson looked a little put out that Peter already knew about the lizards.

"Yeah," he said. "Some loony has gone to every zoo in the city and set all the reptiles free. Crocodiles, snakes, you name it. Look."

Jameson used a remote control to turn on the five

televisions that were set into a wall in his office. Each TV was tuned to a different live news broadcast. People from all parts of the city were talking about their reptile sightings.

One channel was broadcasting a home video filmed only minutes before. The footage was shot from a second floor apartment window and showed the swarm of scaly creatures moving down Madison Avenue. Peter pointed to a figure at the bottom corner of the screen.

"Look, it's the Lizard," Peter said.

Jameson's mouth dropped open as he stared at the giant reptile.

"What's he doing back?" Jameson asked. But he didn't wait for Peter to answer.

"Well, don't just sit there, Parker!" he barked. "Go out and get me some pictures for the front page!"

Just then, one of the assistants from the *Bugle's* photo lab walked into Jameson's office.

"Here are the photos you requested," the assistant

said to Peter, tossing him a package. Luckily for Peter, the assistant had already developed the film of the pictures Spider-Man had taken at Dr. Connors's lab that morning.

"Ask and you shall receive," Peter said to Jameson.

"Don't get smart with me, Parker," Jameson snapped.

As his boss looked through the photos, Peter thought about what was going on. If the news footage he'd just watched was live, that meant someone had set the reptiles free after he'd left the lab.

I have a feeling that someone is a nasty overgrown reptile, Peter thought. *I guess it's time for the Lizard and Spider-Man to meet again.*

Jameson's office phone rang, interrupting Peter's thoughts.

"What?" Jameson snapped into the phone. "Uh-huh. Uh-huh. No kidding . . . What's the address? Right, got it."

"Well," Jameson said, hanging up the phone and turning to Peter, "our friend the Lizard, along with about a thousand assorted reptiles, has just dropped in on an elementary school. He's at Public School 193."

That's Billy Connors's school, Peter thought. *What's the Lizard up to?*

Dr. Connors loved his son, Billy, but he wasn't Dr. Connors at the moment. He was the Lizard, and the Lizard didn't love anyone.

Could this have something to do with that part-lizard formula I saw in Dr. Connors's notebook this morning? Peter wondered. *Surely he wouldn't try the formula on Billy. Or would he?*

"Don't just sit there, Parker," Jameson yelled. "Go see what the Lizard's up to. If you get a photo of him posing with some school kids, I'll give you an extra fifty bucks," Jameson called out, as Peter dashed from the room.

After a quick pit stop in the broom closet to change into his suit, Spider-Man was on his way.

CHAPTER 3

FIVE BURLY COPS BLOCKED THE ENTRANCE to Public School 193 as a large crowd of news reporters and worried parents tried to push their way inside. Keeping a low profile, Spider-Man slipped around to the back of the school. He climbed up the wall and through an open window on the fifth floor.

As soon as he was inside, Spider-Man heard heavy footsteps pounding along the linoleum floor in the corridor outside the classroom. Leaping to the doorway, he saw a row of police officers with tranquilizer guns, aimed and ready. Twenty feet down the hallway, a dozen crocodiles were slithering quickly toward them.

I'm in the mood for a little croc wrestling, Spider-Man thought.

He swung himself over the police officers and landed on top of the biggest crocodile. Spider-Man wrapped a tight band of webbing around its snapping jaws. Then, with two more quick bursts of webbing, he stacked the crocodile on top of another one and bound them both together.

Spider-Man kept firing web blasts as one angry crocodile after another tried to attack him. Before long, he had made two neat piles of tightly wrapped crocs. They drooled through the webbing as their angry eyes followed Spider-Man, but there was nothing they could do.

"Hey, Ms. Gonzalez," Spider-Man called out to Billy's teacher, who was standing behind the line of police officers, "do you think you could use these guys in the science room? Or maybe the cafeteria—there's plenty of meat on them!"

"No, thanks, Spider-Man!" Ms. Gonzalez said. "I think this school has seen enough reptiles for the time being."

I'm in the mood for a little croc wrestling.

Then she continued on in a rush, "You have to find Billy Connors. The giant lizard creature got away, and he took Billy with him."

"Don't worry about a thing, Ms. G," Spider-Man answered. "I'm on it."

Spider-Man left the school and swung his way down Madison Avenue.

There aren't many places a seven-foot lizard can hide, he thought. *Something tells me it's time to see what's going on back at Dr. Connors's lab. I have a hunch the Lizard's planning to use the part-lizard formula on Billy. Talk about double trouble.*

CHAPTER 4

SPIDER-MAN SCALED THE OUTSIDE OF THE science building and peered into Dr. Connors's lab through one of the many holes in the wall. The room was still a mess, but there were no reptiles in sight.

There's no sign of the Lizard or Billy, Spider-Man thought, *but I might as well whip up some Lizard antidote while I'm here. The sooner I can change that monster back into Dr. Connors, the better.*

Spider-Man collected the ingredients to the antidote he'd devised two years ago. He mixed a batch and poured it into several test tubes.

As Spider-Man worked, he thought about the best way to stop the Lizard. The first thing he had to do was get Billy out of the way somehow.

Just as Spider-Man sealed the last tube of antidote, his spider-sense tingled. "The Lizard is coming," he muttered to himself.

Spider-Man scaled the wall and flattened himself against the ceiling. He used his webbing to attach a camera to a light fixture so that he could record for the *Daily Bugle* whatever was about to happen. Spider-Man felt the building tremble as the Lizard made his way up the outside wall. He watched as the top of the Lizard's oversized head appeared. His eyes were bloodshot, and his wide jaw, filled with razor-sharp teeth, was dripping with drool.

I wouldn't want to look at that face in the mirror every morning, thought Spider-Man, as the Lizard climbed inside. He was carrying Billy over his shoulder like a sack of potatoes. He stomped across the floor to the lab table and cleared the surface of glass and debris with one mighty swoop of his arm. Then he dropped Billy onto the table.

"I have a present for you," the Lizard hissed at Billy. "It's a special serum I've created to make you more like me, big and strong. Don't worry, though, you won't turn into a lizard."

"No, Dad, I don't want—" Billy started, but the Lizard cut him off.

"Quiet," the Lizard said. His jaw curved into something like a smile. "Trust me, you will thank me for this later. My serum will give you all the powers of a great reptile, but you'll still look like a human kid. Then you can move among people unnoticed . . . as you destroy them."

Spider-Man had heard enough and was ready to pounce, until he saw the Lizard's hand tighten around the back of Billy's neck.

If I reveal myself now, it could be fatal for Billy, Spider-Man thought. *One extra hard squeeze from the Lizard and Billy will be history.*

Billy was reluctant. "I don't want to hurt anybody," he said.

The Lizard squeezed Billy's neck even tighter. "Lizards are so much better than humans, Billy," he said. "If you take the serum, you'll be able do lots of things humans can't. Life will be a whole lot more fun."

The Lizard let go of Billy's neck and picked him up by the shoulders instead. Then he stepped back and used his tail to smash one of the thick, old-fashioned wooden columns supporting the ceiling. Still carrying Billy, the Lizard moved down the line of columns, breaking one after another as if they were toothpicks. He was obviously trying to show off his powers in an attempt to convince Billy to take the serum.

"See how much fun destruction can be, Billy? Once you get the hang of it, you'll love it. One day you may even be as good at it as I am," the Lizard boasted.

The ceiling groaned and creaked as old boards and plaster struggled to stay upright. If the ceiling fell, Spider-

Man was falling with it. But if he moved now, he was in for a fight—with Billy in the middle of it. Spider-Man couldn't risk that.

"Plus you can climb walls!" the Lizard continued. With Billy slung over his shoulder, he leaped to the far wall and began scaling it as easily as most people walk down the street.

Spider-Man saw his chance. He shot a web-line that caught Billy and swung him across the room, gently dropping him in a corner. Billy crawled behind a column and hid.

The Lizard jumped down from the wall and glared at Spider-Man.

"Okay, Lizard," Spider-Man said, "it's time for you to take your medicine and become a grown-up again."

"Oh, I've got some medicine, Spider-Man," said the Lizard. "But I'm not the one who's going to be taking it." With that, he slammed his tail against one of the last remaining columns. The ceiling creaked and rumbled. Chunks of plaster fell.

He slammed his tail against one of the last remaining columns.

"Run, Billy. Now!" Spider-Man called out. "I'll take care of the overgrown reptile!"

Clouds of plaster dust began to fill the room as parts of the ceiling caved in around them. Spider-Man couldn't see Billy anywhere. In fact, for a moment, as the debris swirled around him, he couldn't see anything at all.

CHAPTER 5

SECONDS PASSED AND THE DUST BEGAN to clear. Spider-Man could see straight through to the sky in places where the ceiling had fallen in. He could also see the Lizard coming straight for him.

Spider-Man shot a web-line that caught the Lizard's head and pulled him forward onto the floor. Making a lasso out of webbing, Spider-Man tied the Lizard's arms behind his scaly back and quickly webbed him to the ground.

"Whoa," Spider-Man said, as the Lizard snapped his jaws furiously, "ever heard of breath mints?" The Lizard hissed at him in response.

"Billy's just a kid," Spider-Man said. "Why do you want

to turn him into a cold-blooded freak? He's got his teenage years for that."

"He's my son, and I'm doing him a favor," said the Lizard, as he fought to break free of Spider-Man's webbing. "Right now Billy is just another foolish human. But if he takes my serum, he'll be like me, maybe even better." With a snap, the Lizard tore open the webbing that had been pinning him down. Within seconds, the Lizard was on his feet. "I'm using him as an experiment, Spider-Man, and you can't stop me."

"I think I'd rather experiment on you, big guy," Spider-Man said. He shot a web-line and pulled himself toward the opposite wall, catching the Lizard with his feet as he went. Spider-Man slammed the overgrown reptile hard against the bricks, and then shot webbing into his eyes, blinding him temporarily.

Just then, Billy cried out. Backed up against the column, he was surrounded by five Komodo dragons, snarling and hissing at him. *The Lizard must have summoned them,* Spider-Man thought. He fired a web-line that lifted Billy six feet off the ground and webbed him to a column, out of range of the dragons.

"Enough talk!" the Lizard hissed. By this time he had managed to remove the webbing from his face. "Lizards eat spiders for breakfast, and I'm hungry!"

The Lizard swung his powerful tail, whacking Spider-Man in the stomach and sending him flying into the far wall. Spider-Man slumped to the ground, motionless.

"I'm going to enjoy squishing you, Spider-Man," the Lizard hissed, as he stomped over to him.

In a flash, Spider-Man jumped to his feet. "But that wouldn't be nearly as much fun as fitting you for a new web-suit," he said, wrapping the Lizard in webbing around and around until he was covered from his claw-feet to his snout.

"See, that looks good on you, but maybe we need to let it out a little at the waist," Spider-Man said, as he reached for one of the tubes filled with antidote.

As Spider-Man turned back to the Lizard, he heard the snap of breaking wood. The Lizard had torn himself free and was pulling a column from its moorings top and bottom. As Spider-Man ducked away from the chunks of falling plaster, the Lizard smashed the top of the heavy column on Spider-Man's head. Spider-Man went down as more plaster and dust floated around him.

Spider-Man got to his feet, still a little woozy. The Lizard lunged at him, and they both struggled to gain control. As they wrestled, the Lizard slowly backed Spider-Man toward the hole in the wall. If he pushed Spider-Man through, it would be a five-story drop to the pavement below.

"I think it's time for you to take a little trip!" growled the Lizard, as he shoved Spider-Man through the hole.

With Spider-Man gone, the Lizard turned back to Billy. "The hardest part will be taking the serum," he said. "But you'll soon realize it was worth it. We'll be a team, and no one will be able to stop us. Not even Spider-Man."

Billy thought for a minute. He was a smart kid, and he'd seen what the Lizard had just done to Spider-Man. It seemed like he didn't really have a choice.

"Okay, I guess so," said Billy. The Lizard ripped apart the webbing that held Billy to the column, letting him drop to the floor.

"Hurry up and drink this," the Lizard said, thrusting a steel test tube at Billy's mouth.

As soon as Billy swallowed the contents of the tube, a look of pain crossed his face. He bent over, clutching his stomach as if he were about to be sick. Just as quickly, though, his expression changed. Now he seemed excited.

"This stuff is awesome!" Billy said. Drool dripped from his teeth, which were a tiny bit longer and sharper than before. He walked over to a wall, made a fist, and punched a hole right through the bricks. Next, he flexed his knees and leaped all the way across the room in one go. With a tremendous thump, he kicked over the lab table.

"What can we do now?" Billy shouted. "I want to

have some fun!" Billy had definitely changed. His nose had lengthened into a small snout, his eyes were bulging, and his skin was now light green and a little bit scaly.

"Son," the Lizard said, "there is so much we can do in this big city full of disgusting humans. We're going to start causing some real trouble for the citizens of New York. How does that sound?"

"Cool!" Billy said. "Let's go!" They ran from the room just as Spider-Man, who hadn't fallen very far before catching himself with a web-line, pulled himself back inside.

CHAPTER 6

PETER WAS WOKEN EARLY THE NEXT morning by the loud ring of his cell phone. It was Jameson calling from his office at the *Daily Bugle.*

Let me guess, there's another big story breaking? So what else is new? Peter thought groggily. Spider-Man had spent most of the previous night searching for the Lizard and Billy, with no luck.

Peter slowly threw back the covers and got out of bed. He wanted nothing more than to be out looking for the Lizard and Billy, but he had to show up for his job, even if only for a few minutes.

Looks like I won't be starting that term paper that's due

next week anytime soon, Peter thought. *Maybe I can tell the professor that a lizard ate my homework.*

"Big news, Parker," Jameson said, as soon as Peter walked into his boss's office at the *Bugle*. "Apparently Spider-Man broke into the Holbein building yesterday."

What? Peter thought. *I was nowhere near Holbein yesterday. Someone must be impersonating me as Spider-Man. That's all I need right now.*

"I knew that spider was no good," growled Jameson. "Anyway, what have you got for me on the Lizard story? Show me something new." Peter uploaded the photos he'd taken at the lab to Jameson's computer. He'd have to worry about the impersonator later.

Jameson looked at the slide show of photos, but kept glancing over at the televisions on his wall. The Spider-Man story was breaking news on every channel. Jameson was unimpressed with Peter's photos until he saw what the Lizard had done to Billy.

"This is front-page stuff," Jameson said, rubbing his hands together in glee. "He's turned his son into a lizard! Now we've got not one but two crazy lizards making news all over the city." Jameson looked like he'd just gotten the best Christmas present ever.

"I've got it!" Jameson yelled. "We'll call him Lil' Lizard. It sounds like a rapper, it's easy to remember, and it'll sell papers!" He picked up the phone and barked, "Send our best writer in here. I need a story fast. We've got something for the evening edition!"

Peter didn't say anything. He liked the Connorses. It was hard to think of this as just another way to sell papers. He had to find the Lizard and Billy and get them to take the antidote before they caused too much destruction.

Jameson turned up the volume on one of the televisions.

"Kelly Cheng here for Channel Twelve News. We are live outside the Chocolate Factory where well-known villain, the Lizard, and a young, unknown accomplice have taken over the entire store. There are at least fifty people inside, and it's not known what . . ."

"Okay, Parker," Jameson said, still staring at the screen, "you know the drill. Go get the pictures!"

But Peter was already gone. At the first mention of the Lizard, he was out the door and racing to the bathroom to change into his Spider-Man suit.

CHAPTER 7

SPIDER-MAN LANDED ON THE ROOF OF the Chocolate Factory and lowered himself into the store through a manhole. Inside, twenty police officers were lined up near the entrance.

Best of luck, guys, Spider-Man thought, *but I think it's going to take more than that to stop the Lizard.*

On the opposite side of the store, the Lizard towered over a group of terrified customers, who were huddled together in a corner.

Snarling and spitting, the Lizard used his tail to send display tables flying. Splinters of wood and showers of candy rained down on the crowd. With one swipe of his enormous arm, he shattered a couple of the candy tubes that ran from the ceiling to the floor. The ground was thick with crushed chocolates.

A police officer rushed at him, but the Lizard just punched a hole right through the officer's safety shield, striking his visor and knocking him to the ground.

Spider-Man positioned himself so he had a clear shot at the Lizard. *I need to put the big guy out of action for a minute so I can get the customers out of here,* he thought.

Unfortunately, the Lizard wasn't the only reptile with anger issues that Spider-Man had to worry about.

"Hey, Dad, look at me!" Billy shouted. "Look how high up I am!" He was about forty feet off the ground, at the top of a plastic tube full of red gummy candy. He smashed open the plastic tube, pulled out a handful of candy, and stuffed it into his drooling mouth.

"Stop playing and start breaking things," shouted the Lizard. "This isn't a game!"

Spider-Man fired two long webs at the Lizard, wrapping

"Give it up! We've got you covered!"

his wrists together. He then lassoed the reptile's huge feet together and pulled him over onto his face.

Visors pulled down and shields up, the police rushed in again and formed a human wall around the fallen Lizard.

"Give it up! We've got you covered!" one officer shouted.

Not quite, thought Spider-Man. "Heads up, you guys!" he called out.

Billy was directly above them, hanging from a candy tube. With a growl, he pulled the tube loose from the ceiling. Thousands of pounds of broken plastic and sticky candy rained down onto the police officers. Above them, Billy jumped from tube to tube, cracking each one and pouring candy down onto the people below.

Spider-Man web-slung around the room, creating safety nets for the remaining candy tubes. Now, even if Billy broke the tubes, the candy would be caught by webbing. But Spider-Man had bigger problems to deal with than candy.

The Lizard had freed himself. Spider-Man could see him

moving behind a giant mound of gumballs. Within seconds, the Lizard had leaped over the pile of candy and stood face-to-face with Spider-Man.

"Let's settle this once and for all, Spider-Man!" he said.

"I can't think of anything I'd like more," Spidey answered. He crouched down, ready to charge at the Lizard. Just then, Billy called out to him.

"Hey, Spider-Man, you better catch this guy or he might get hurt," Billy said, as he tossed into the air one of the police officers who had been stuck under the candy. Instinctively, Spider-Man leaped up and caught the officer.

That was all the distraction the Lizard and Billy needed to make their getaway. They ran for the door, shouting insults back over their shoulders.

"Have a sweet time cleaning up the mess, Spidey," the Lizard said. "Hope to see you again soon."

Once again, the two monstrous creatures were loose in the city.

CHAPTER 8

SPIDER-MAN BARRELED OUT OF THE FRONT entrance of the Chocolate Factory. He was just in time to see Billy disappear around the corner of the block up ahead. Shooting a web-line at the nearest light pole, Spider-Man swung up to the roof of the building at the end of the street.

From his vantage point on the roof, Spider-Man could see the Lizard and Billy making their way to the Queensboro Bridge.

Oh, man, not the bridge, thought Spider-Man. *They'll have a field day with the rush hour traffic up there.*

Spider-Man used his webbing to create a giant slingshot. He centered himself inside the slingshot, stepped back as far as he could, and then shot himself like a rocket through the air toward the bridge.

Once he was over the top of the bridge, Spider-Man shot a web-line across to one of the tall metal pillars in the middle and pulled himself down to the railing. He was only a few seconds ahead of the Lizard and Billy, who were almost on the bridge.

Game on, thought Spider-Man, as he whipped through the air toward the lizards. *I'll knock the Lizard off the side of the bridge and grab Billy.*

The Lizard's back was turned, but Billy saw Spider-Man coming.

"Watch out!" Billy yelled to the Lizard, as Spider-Man struck the oversized reptile square in the chest with all the force of a speeding car. The Lizard went flying high into the air and over the side of the bridge. Seizing his chance, Spider-Man scooped up Billy and swung out over the water.

Billy squirmed and scratched at Spider-Man as they swung from the bridge. Down below, Spider-Man caught a

Game on!

glimpse of the Lizard hitting the water.

He'll be out of there before long, thought Spider-Man. *I don't have much time.*

Spider-Man pulled out the tube of antidote. "Billy, buddy, you have to take this," he said. "I know you don't want to, but life as a good guy has many more perks than the villain business."

Billy growled, looking even more like the hideous Lizard than he did an hour ago. Spider-Man tried to push the antidote into Billy's mouth, but Billy chomped and bit at him with his sharp teeth.

A gigantic thud above announced that the Lizard was back. He stomped across the bridge, ignoring the cars that swerved and skidded to avoid hitting him.

"I don't think so, Spider-Man," the Lizard called out. "Billy likes being a powerful reptile. Together we're going to destroy you and all the other warm-bloods."

The Lizard stopped and looked around. "On second thought, I'll get to you in a minute, Spider-Man," he said. "I don't want to waste this opportunity for destruction."

Billy laughed and spat at Spider-Man. "Go for it, Dad," he shouted up to the Lizard.

The Lizard reached out and grabbed a passing car. It was a large jeep, but the Lizard picked it up as if it were a toy. Spider-Man could see the looks of terror on the faces of the people inside. He pulled himself and Billy back up onto the bridge. As they landed, the Lizard tossed the jeep straight up into the air.

As the jeep started its fall, Spider-Man spun a web that spanned the width of the bridge. The jeep landed softly on the web-net, and Spider-Man could see that everyone inside was safe.

The Lizard continued grabbing and tossing cars as they screeched to a halt in front of his massive figure. Spider-Man reinforced the web to hold the weight of the cars and then turned toward the Lizard. Billy was back at his father's side.

"See you later, Spider-Man," the Lizard said. "We've got bigger things to do than play with a few cars!" Billy and the Lizard leaped over the side of the bridge and disappeared.

Back on the bridge, the traffic was in chaos. Spider-Man started to untangle the piled-up cars, while at the same time directing the oncoming vehicles. By the time the police arrived, the Lizard and Billy were long gone.

Time to stock up on web-fluid, Spider-Man thought. *I've already gone through a month's supply cleaning up after those scaly beasts.*

Spider-Man landed in the alley behind his building and changed into his street clothes. Walking around to the front entrance, he picked up a copy of the *Daily Bugle.*

NEW VILLAIN IN TOWN: LIL' LIZARD screamed the headline.

Jameson sure doesn't waste any time, thought Peter. *At least now people will know what to look out for. Not that the lizards are hard to miss.*

Once he was inside his apartment, Peter quickly created enough fluid to fill all of his web-shooters.

As Peter worked, he thought about how he was going to get Billy and the Lizard to take the antidote once he found them again. He remembered the police officers and their tranquilizer darts at Public School 193. He had an idea.

For the first time all day, Peter actually smiled. He rifled through his desk, looking for the equipment that he used to make his web-launchers. For twenty minutes he tinkered with the antidote and a new model web-shooter he'd been developing. When he was finished, Peter again slipped on his Spider-Man suit and set out to find the lizards.

By the time Spider-Man reached Midtown, his spider-sense was tingling. There was trouble downtown. Spider-Man web-swung down the Avenue of the Americas toward Little Italy. His spider-sense went into overdrive as he approached a large, crowded street fair.

Why do I get the feeling that I won't be having any fun at this fair? thought Spider-Man, as he swung farther south over the packed streets below.

CHAPTER 9

SPIDER-MAN KNEW THE SAN GENNARO STREET festival well. His uncle Ben had taken Peter every year when Peter was a kid. The fair was full of old-fashioned rides like the Ferris wheel, Tilt-A-Whirl, spinning teacups, and bumper cars. People came from all over the city, and the mood was always festive.

Spider-Man scanned the scene from the roof of an adjacent building. The fair looked almost exactly the same as he remembered it, except that this year only two of the fairgoers were having fun. The Lizard and Billy were leaping from ride to ride, playing games and knocking over stands when they didn't win. They'd already done a lot of damage.

A couple hundred fairgoers huddled in one corner of the lot. Others were trapped on the Ferris wheel. For the moment, the Lizard and Billy weren't paying any attention to the crowd. But the only exit to the fair was several yards away from the scared throng, and no one dared move.

I have to get these people out of here before I can deal with the lizards, Spider-Man thought. He shot a web-line at the fence next to the crowd and, with a tug, pulled it down. The fairgoers scrambled over the broken fence to freedom. That left only the people trapped on the Ferris wheel.

Spider-Man lowered himself on a web-line into the fair as the Lizard strutted over to the old man who was operating the Ferris wheel. The Lizard picked up the old man by the shirt collar and tossed him aside. Seizing the gearshift, the Lizard made the ride go faster, obviously enjoying the fear he saw on the riders' faces as the rickety old machine picked up speed.

Not far away, Billy was riding the bumper cars, slamming into the empty cars around him at full speed.

"Come over here," the Lizard called out to him. "There are people to play with on this ride." He brought the Ferris

Spider-Man had no choice but to save the riders.

wheel to a stop, and Billy ran to him. Billy's face was now more reptilian than human.

Billy leaped onto the wheel and began climbing the ride. The old steel frame creaked and groaned as he pulled himself up, punching cars and scaring the trapped passengers along the way.

Spider-Man swung himself to the top of the Tilt-A-Whirl, which was right next to the Ferris wheel. Billy had jumped onto one of the cars and was making it rock wildly. The passengers screamed as Billy tried to break the bolts that held the car to the wheel. Spider-Man shot a stream of webbing, binding the car in place. Another web blast caught Billy around the waist, and with a quick jerk on the web-line, Spider-Man sent him spinning to the ground.

Suddenly, the Ferris wheel began to turn again, first at a normal speed, then faster and faster. The metal safety belt in one of the cars snapped from the force, and two passengers went flying into the air. Spider-Man shot a safety net, cradling them as he lowered them onto the teacup ride.

Spider-Man dropped down to where the Lizard stood with one of his knobby claws holding the accelerator gearshift all the way to the left for maximum speed. Spider-Man shot a triple-thick strand of webbing at the gearshift and yanked hard to the right. The wheel began to slow down.

The Lizard, pulling even harder, snapped Spider-Man's webbing and moved the shift back into high speed. Behind them, Billy's laughter rang out as he watched the frightened passengers. Spider-Man shot more webbing and tugged backward on the gearshift, inching closer and closer to the Lizard with each step.

Spider-Man could see the motor of the Ferris wheel. It had gigantic metal wheels with huge teeth, all spinning wildly to keep the wheel moving at such a high speed. If the Lizard took one or two steps backward, he'd be caught in the gears.

Minced Lizard meat, anyone? thought Spider-Man.

Spider-Man shot a web-line at the Lizard's feet, binding them together. The Lizard teetered briefly and went flying backward into the swiftly spinning gears.

"Take that, Lizard lips," Spider-Man said. He walked over to the gearshift and yanked on it, bringing the wheel to a complete stop.

Turning back to face the Lizard, Spider-Man saw the over-sized reptile walking toward him.

What? I thought only cats had nine lives. How can he be unharmed? Spider-Man wondered.

But then Spider-Man realized the Lizard was walking slowly and seemed a little bit wobbly on his feet. His gigantic tail had been cut off at the tip, throwing him off balance.

The Lizard hissed at Spider-Man, but then turned around and began to laugh as the tip of a new tail emerged. Within seconds, it had grown into a complete tail, identical to the old one.

Wow, thought Spider-Man, *that is pretty cool.*

The Lizard grabbed one corner of the old Ferris wheel's steel base and lifted it up. The whole ride teetered and the passengers screamed as the Lizard gave it a push, causing the ride to fall toward the ground. Spider-Man had no choice but to save the riders, and that meant letting the Lizard go—for now.

"Come on," the Lizard called to Billy, "we've got work to do."

As they ran from the park, Spider-Man saw Billy drop something. It was a map of the New York City subway.

CHAPTER 10

SPIDER-MAN MADE HIS WAY THROUGH THE tunnels that made up New York City's underground train system. There were no signs of the Lizard or Billy anywhere, but his spider-sense told him they were somewhere within the dark maze.

Finally, at eight o'clock the next morning, Spider-Man's spider-sense led him to the Broadway-Nassau station. Once there, the announcement system clicked on and a distinctive voice spoke.

"We apologize for the delay. Power will be restored shortly and this train will be leaving in a few minutes."

Spider-Man heard relieved commuters talking on the platform. Spider-Man wasn't feeling quite so reassured.

The voice that had made the announcement belonged to the Lizard.

As Spider-Man walked deeper into the tunnel, following his spider-sense, he passed old steel columns and the power boxes that kept the electricity flowing and the subway cars moving. Eventually, he heard the Lizard and Billy ahead and moved carefully toward them.

"This is a perfect plan, Billy. The whole city is going to come to a stop," the Lizard said.

Billy laughed. "I can't believe it's going to be this easy," he said. "It took us no time to move the tracks closer to each other. It's just like when I play with my electric train set."

"The best part is that this is only the first of all the crashes," said the Lizard. "We've moved the tracks in at least fifty or sixty places. Once we get the trains running again, there'll be mass destruction. It will be glorious!"

"Hurry up and turn on the power again," said Billy. "It's time to play smash 'em up."

I knew the Lizard was cold-blooded, thought Spider-Man,

but this is heartless even for him. Thousands of people could
be killed.

The Lizard and Billy had lifted the metal from two tracks and replanted them so they now crossed over. If a pair of trains ran side by side on these tracks, they would definitely collide. Billy was standing at the intersection of the two tracks, exactly where the trains would smash into each other.

"This one is just for fun, really," said Billy. "I just want to see the two trains crash!" But the Lizard was too busy rewiring the power source for the whole subway system to pay attention to Billy. With a few swift connections, all the trains, which had been stopped in Manhattan stations all night, opened their doors and let on thousands of passengers. Then their doors closed, and the trains began to pick up speed.

The rumble of trains thundered along the tracks the lizards had rerouted. Two trains came into view. They were moving at such high speeds that the noise was deafening. Within moments they were very close to meeting at their new intersection, where Billy was still standing on the tracks.

Why isn't Billy moving out of the way? Spider-Man wondered. Then he saw that Billy's foot was stuck under the metal track. He was struggling to get free, but he couldn't lift the track on his own.

Billy didn't seem too worried, though. "Hey, look at me! I'm going to get caught in a train crash, and I'll grow a totally new me!" he called out.

But Spider-Man knew this wasn't true.

The Lizard knew this, too. Using his powerful legs, the Lizard launched himself at Billy, who was still standing in the danger zone, laughing and showing a full set of pointy teeth.

The trains were seconds from crashing when Spider-Man saw his chance. As the Lizard pulled Billy free, Spider-Man shot a web-line at the power switch, shutting down the oncoming trains, which slowly screeched to a halt only inches from each other and from the two monstrous lizards.

Spider-Man quickly shot a wall of webbing around the lizards, binding them together.

"This is the end of the line for you, my friends," Spider-Man said to them.

Spider-Man ran to the transmitter box and dismantled the rest of the Lizard's connections. Throughout the station, he heard trains begin to slow down and eventually stop. With that major crisis averted, he had one last thing to do.

Enraged that his plan had failed, the Lizard had already ripped free of the webbing. As he stood up and prepared to charge, Spider-Man inserted one of the antidote dart cartridges that he had made earlier into his web-shooter. When the Lizard was within a few feet of him, Spider-Man shot an antidote dart into the leathery skin of his thick neck.

The effect was almost instantaneous. The scaling, the teeth, the evil expression all slipped away, and in their place was Dr. Connors. When he saw his reptile son, recognizable only because of his school clothes, Dr. Connors couldn't believe his eyes.

"Billy, what's happened to you?" His son was stomping angrily back and forth between the two tunnels, furious that he hadn't gotten to see the spectacular train crash. He wouldn't even speak to his now-human dad. When he saw Spider-Man, Billy flew into a rage. He threw himself through the air, teeth and claws bared, ready to fight.

Spider-Man was ready. He aimed his antidote dart cartridge at Billy and fired. The dart hit Billy in his shoulder. The antidote worked, and seconds later, Billy was a normal kid again. He was just a scared little boy in a dark subway tunnel, until he saw Dr. Connors.

"Dad," he said, "what's going on?"

Dr. Connors scooped Billy up in his arms and hugged him.

"Billy," he said, "we have a lot to talk about. I'm so sorry for what I did to you."

While Spider-Man helped subway riders out of the cars, father and son sat talking quietly together.

Billy's a good kid, Spider-Man thought. *Maybe one day he'll be a great scientist like his father. I hope I can spend more time with them both in the future. But if I never see the Lizard or Lil' Lizard again, it will be too soon.*